By Agnes N. Hopps

AuthorHouse™
1663 Liberty Drive
Bloomington, IN 47403
www.authorhouse.com
Phone: 1-800-839-8640

First published by AuthorHouse 09/29/2011

ISBN: 978-1-4634-0672-1 (sc)

Library of Congress Control Number: 2011908644

Printed in the United States of America

Once there was a small pretty Island. An Island is a piece of land with water all around it. And the only way to get on and off the island is by boat. The little island was east of the big cities on Big Land.

And the Sun would rise over the island every morning. And set over the big city every night.

This little island was called Happy Island. And on this island there live a little boy name Jordan. Jordan was a happy little boy and was very smart. He loved his little island and didn't want to go to see what was in the Big City, like his friends.

They all wanted to get on the big boats, just to go see what was in the big city. They had tried to swim to the Big land, but it was too far.

Happy Island was a great place to live because everything you wanted was there. But school was the best of all. For every good mark or star you got in school, you would get a time out to play on the beach.

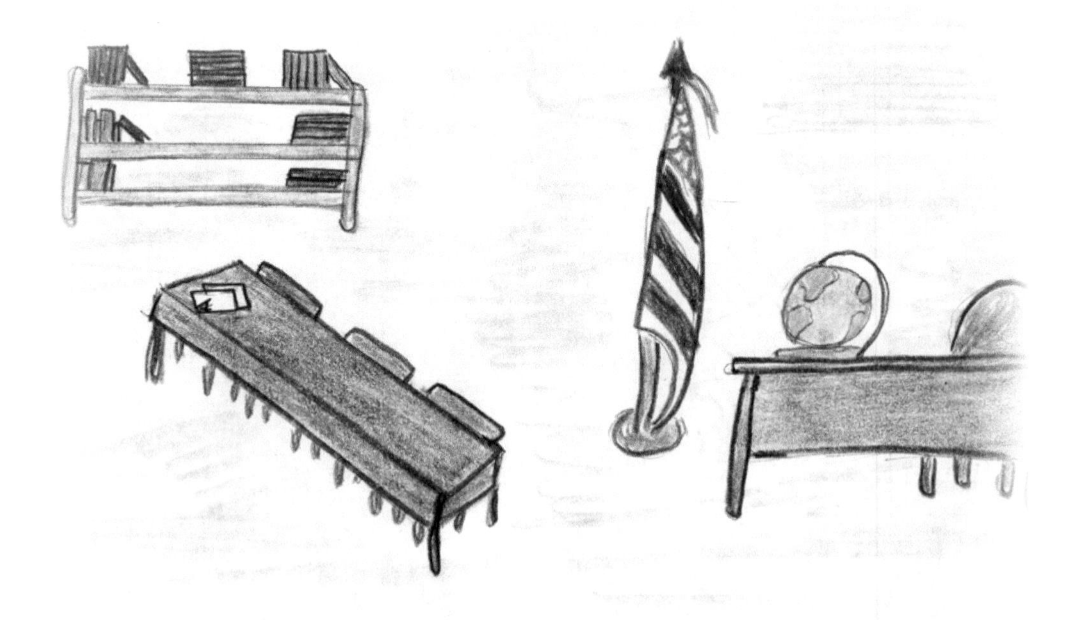

And Jordan was very good in school and got a lot of good marks and stars. So he was on the beach all the time. And he loved it. He did all his homework, all his class work and he did his best and he did it right.

One day Jordan was very, very good in school and his marks were very, very good. He did all of his homework, all of his class work and he had help his friends with their school work too.

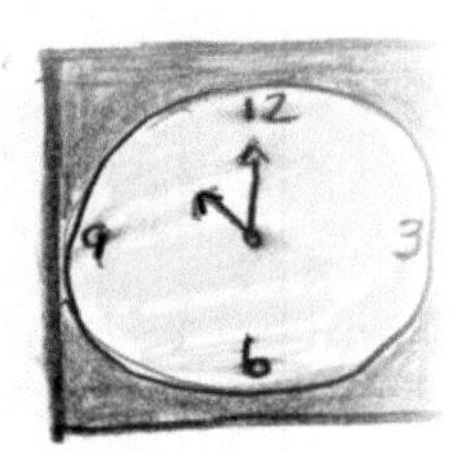

"You have been a very good boy today, Jordan" said his teacher.

"After lunch you can go to the beach and play until the bell ring and it is time to go home."

Jordan was very happy. It was a pretty day and he want to be on the beach today.

"Jordan, maybe you should take a nap first?" his teacher said.

“No, thank you”, said Jordan, “I don’t need a nap.”

So after lunch he closed his books and went out the door down to the beach. This was right out in front of the little school.

Jordan sat down on the warm sand and took off his shoes so that his feet could feel the warm sand. He looked around at the pretty blue water.

“I should go swimming today,” he through. “Maybe I’ll swim all the way around the island.”

But no one had ever swum all the way around the island, it was too far. He laid back to rest for just a second.

He looked around and saw a man putting up a sign. The man had put up the same sign down the beach.

"What does it say," Jordan wonders.

“Mister, what do the sign say” he asked?

“Come closer and see,” the man said.

“I’m sorry I can not come closer I’ve have to stay in front of the school or I will not be able to come out and play again.” Jordan always obeys the rules.

“It says Dolphin, Shark, and Killer Whale,” the man yells back at Jordan,

“I have to go. I have a lot more signs to put up”. “Mister what did you say?” Jordan asked, “I didn’t hear you.”

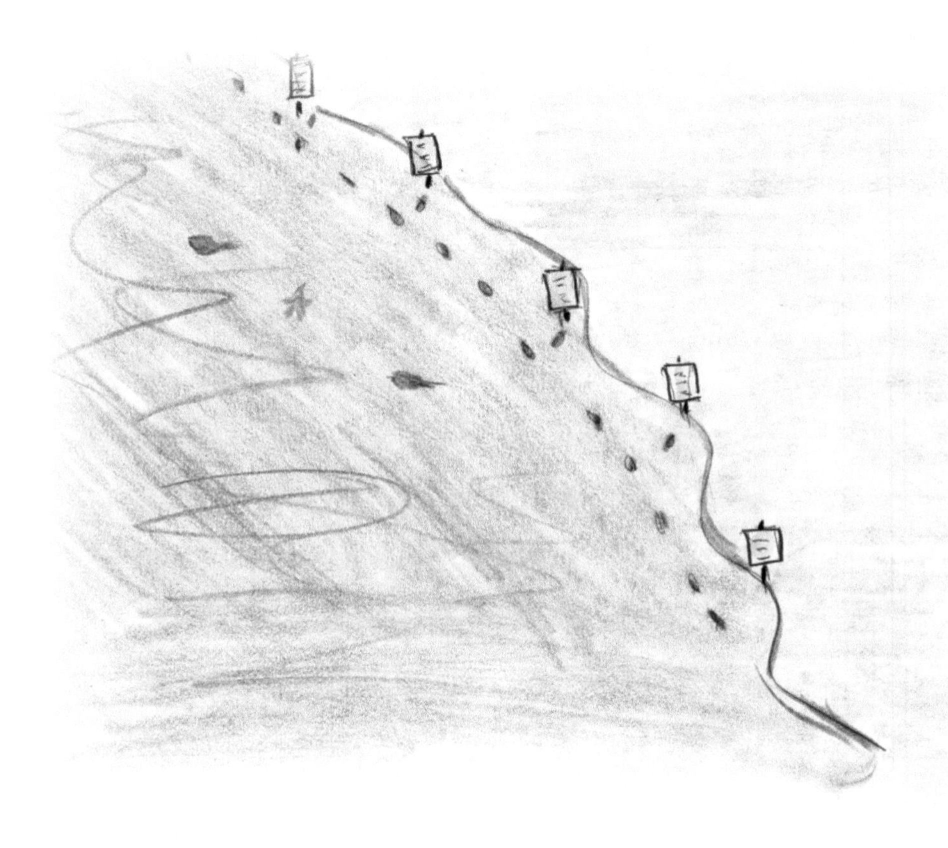

“Dolphin, Shark, and Killer Whale,” the man yells back as he walked up the beach putting up more signs.

“Did he say, Dolphin, shark, and killer whale,” Jordan said out loud.

"In our waters? There aren't any dolphins or sharks or killer whales in our water. This is a happy island with happy waters no dolphin or shark or killer whale in our waters".

Jordan sat up and watched the man put up signs down the beach. Jordan smile.

"This is a big joke; someone is playing a joke on us."

Click! Click! “No joke Jordan, here we are,” Clicked the dolphin.

“Who said that,” Jordan said.

“Here to your left.” clicked the dolphin.

“I’ve come to play with you. You see I was a very good dolphin is dolphin school and I have the rest of the day off too,” clicked the dolphin.

Jordan looked to his left and there to his left was a dolphin jumping in and out of the water.

“You are a dolphin, and you talk,” Jordan said.

“Beep! Beep! Well we all talk in our own way.” beeps the killer whale.

“Who said that”, asked Jordan. “I did, to your right,” said the killer whale. Jordan looked to his right and saw a big killer whale, blowing water from his head.

"You are a whale what are you doing here?" said Jordan.

"You see I was good in whale school. So I came to play with you too."

"Oh my", said Jordan, "You talk too."

"Hiss! Hiss! He is not so smart everything talks, in their own way. Why does he keep saying YOU TALK?"

"Who said that," looking from his right to his left.

"Here it is me, to your front," the shark hissed and smile, "and before you ask, yes I am a shark and yes I was good in shark school and yes I came to play with you also."

“But children can’t play with sharks,” said Jordan.

“Why not,” hiss the shark, “I like to play”.

“But you may eat me,” said Jordan.

“I’ve had lunch, thank very much and little boys were not on the menu. I just want to play,” hissed the shark.

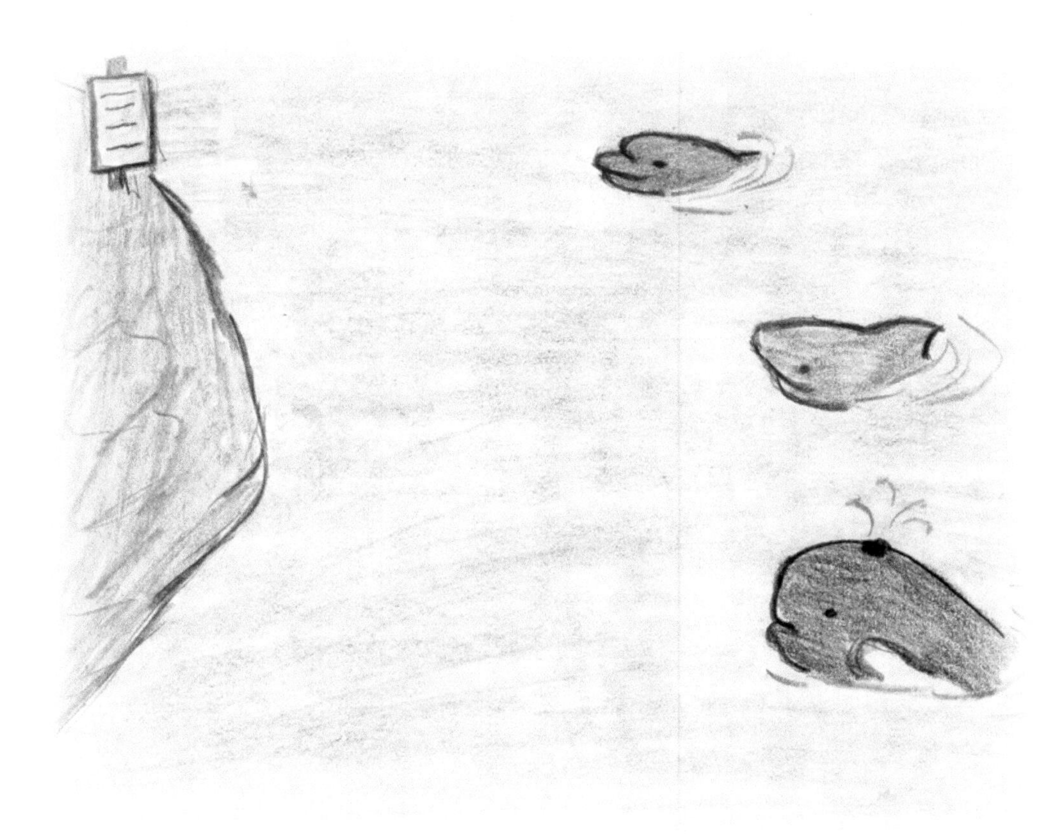

"**Come** in the water I want you to play with me," said the dolphin as he jumped high in and out of the water to his left.

"No, No, come in the water and play with me," beep the killer whale as he blew water high up out of his head.

“You don’t want to play with them, come in the water and play with me,” hiss the shark in front of him.

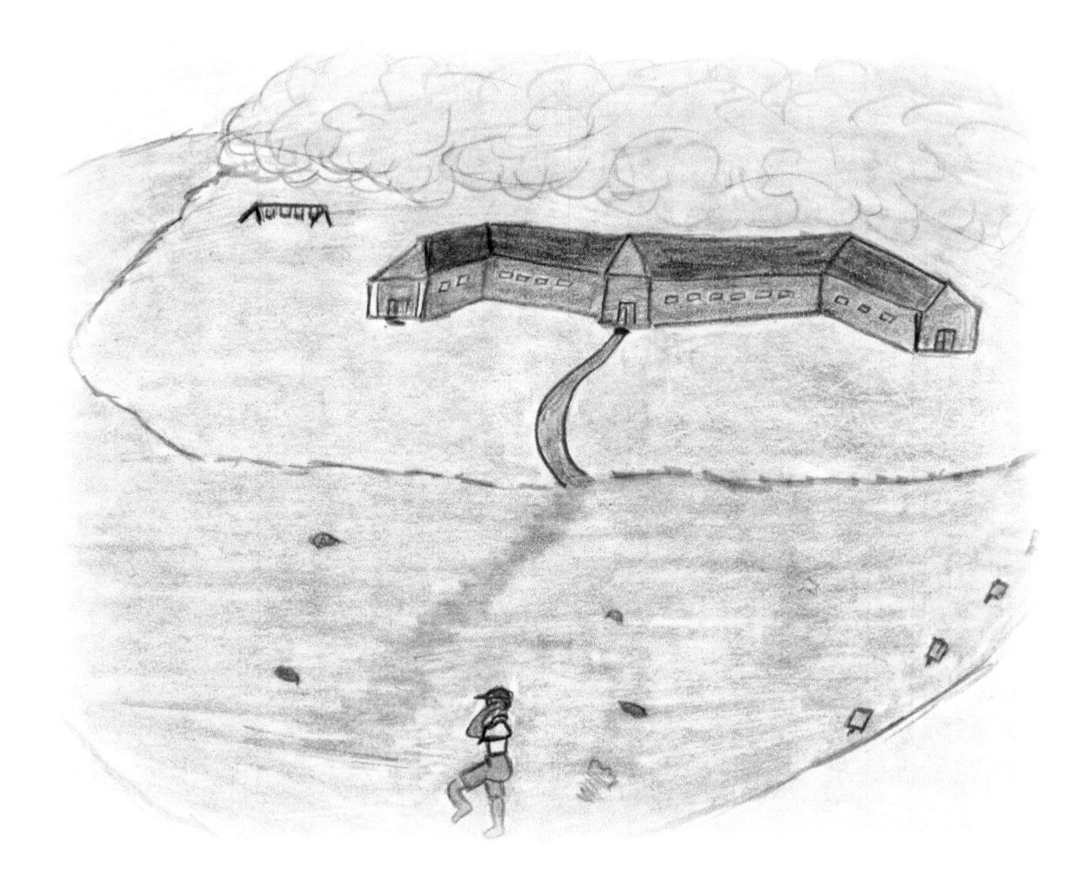

They all kept calling him and calling him.

"JORDAN JORDAN COME IN THE WATER AND PLAY," they said, louder and louder. Jordan put his hand on his ears and ran back to the school house.

He ran back to the school to tell the teacher; that there was a dolphin, a shark and a killer whale in the water at the beach.

"That is silly Jordan," the teacher said, "There are no dolphins and sharks and killer whales in our water at our beach."

“No just one dolphin and one shark and one killer whale and yes they are in our water,” Jordan said.

“Calm down Jordan,” the teacher said, “you can stay in the class with us. You do have a little play time left; you can go back to the beach and you’ll see that there is no dolphin, shark, or killer whale”.

Very sad Jordan walked back to the beach.

"Are you back to play with us?" they ask. He sat on the beach and look around.

"What do you want," asked Jordan.

"All we want to do is to play with the little boy who was so good in school and so smart the he got the day off to play. Because we were good in school we got the day off too so we came to play with you."

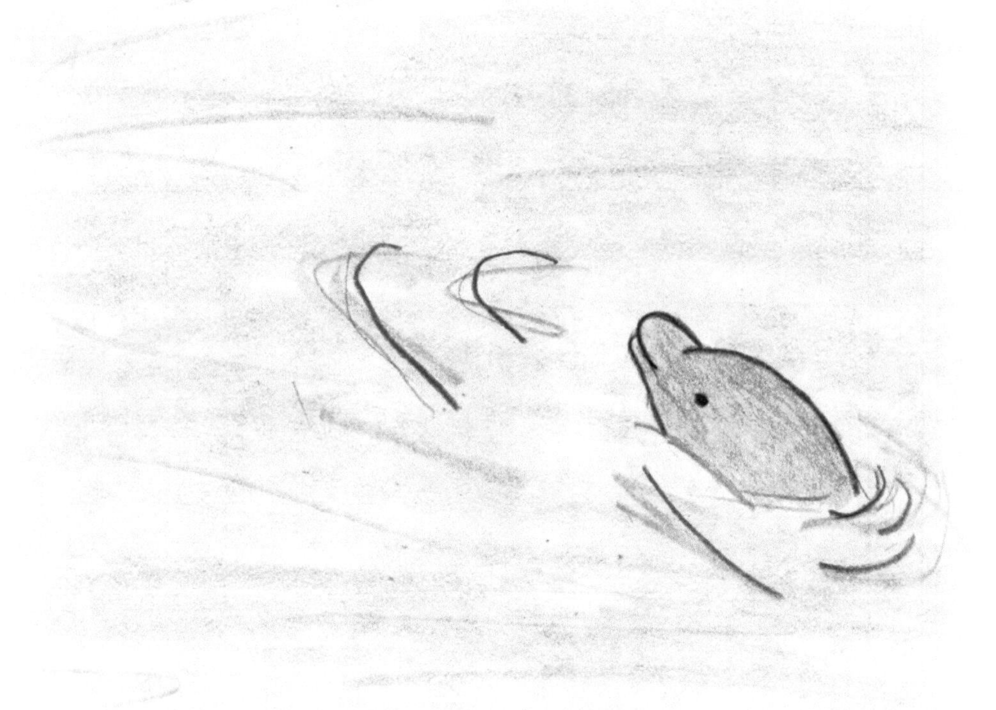

"But won't you and the others eat me," asked Jordan.

"Why would we eat you? We just wanted to play," said the shark.

"We can all play together," said the dolphin. Jordan though about it for a time, than he walked in the water.

The dolphin said, “Get on my back and hold on tight to my fin. I can jump high and dive in the water. Hold on!” The dolphin jump high in and out of the water. And Jordan laughed and laughed. This, he thought was great fun.

The shark yelled, “come on, come on it is my turn to play.” He told Jordan to hold on tighter because he could swim so fast that all the water will fly high up beside him. Jordan held on very tight and the shark swam so fast it felt like riding in a race car. Now this, he thought, was great fun.

The killer whale yelled "It's my turn, my turn to play. Get on my back and sit on my blow hole, on my head," he told Jordan. The whale took a big drink of water. He let him set on his water hole on his head and blew the water and shooting Jordan high up in the air and down again.

Jordan landed on the whale’s big soft head. Jordan thought, this is really great fun. He was having so much fun that he did not hear the school bell ring.

“Jordan, Jordan, wake up,” the teacher said as she shook him lightly. “You should have taken a nap you been asleep the whole time and you didn’t get to play.” Jordan looked around and there were no signs on the beach.

He looks in the water there was no dolphin to his left and no shark in front and no killer whale to the right.

"I'm sorry you did not get to play but it is time to go home," said his teacher. "You look like you were having a great dream."

Jordan smile to himself. “I had fun,” he said to himself, “Lots of fun.” He looked off in the distance. He could see three fins, waving goodbye. He waved goodbye to his friends, the dolphin, the shark and the killer whale.

THE END

Printed in the United States
by Baker & Taylor Publisher Services